By Ruth Anfinson Bures
Illustrated by Amy Kleinhans

I'm so glad there's someone who thinks that I'm okay,
Who's seen my good and bad days and loves me anyway, because . . .

Sometimes I feel ANGRY when life just isn't fair.
I want to shout! I want to scream and grab something to TEAR!

I grumble and I sputter.

I snarl and GNASH MY TEETH.

I fume and fuss and fret, slam doors and STAMP MY FEET!

But when someone who **loves me** says, "You're really mad today. Please tell me why. What happened to make you feel this way?" Then **I feel safe** to talk about whatever's on my mind. I get my angry feelings out and let them **all unwind.**

Sometimes I feel stupid. Can't do things right at all.
My fumbly, stumbly, bumbly brain must need an overhaul.

Sometimes I feel hopeless. Don't like myself one bit.
My ears, my hair, my feet, my nose, my PARTS don't seem to fit.

But when someone who **loves me** says, "You're really blue today. Please tell me why. What happened to make you feel this way?"
Then **I feel safe** to talk about whatever's on my mind.
I get my gloomy feelings out and let them **all unwind.**

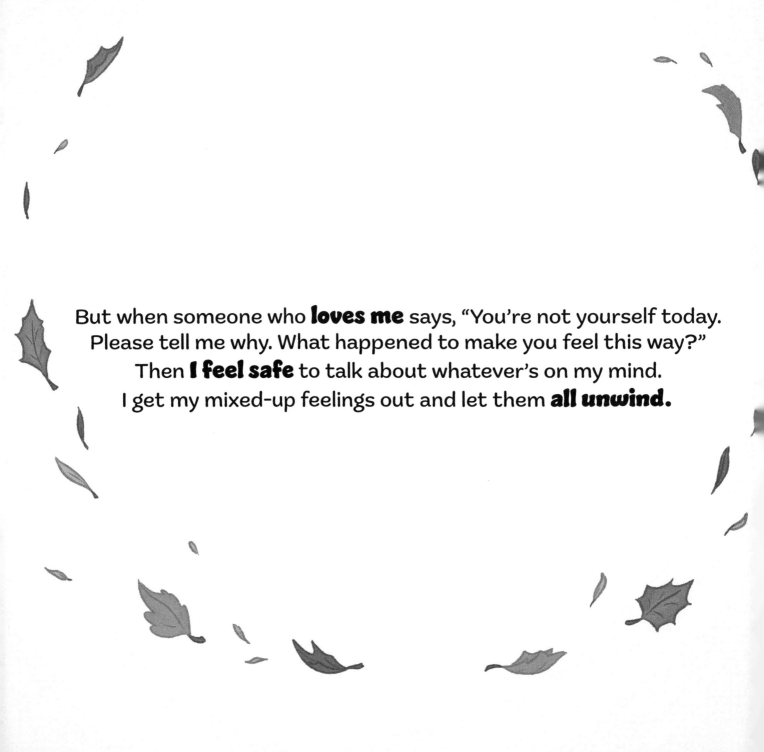

But when someone who **loves me** says, "You're not yourself today. Please tell me why. What happened to make you feel this way?" Then **I feel safe** to talk about whatever's on my mind. I get my mixed-up feelings out and let them **all unwind.**

Sometimes **I GET WORRIED** over bad news that I hear.
The scary things that happen **FILL MY THINKING UP WITH FEAR.**

And when there is a **SQUABBLE** where **PEOPLE DISAGREE,**
The angry words and moves and sounds can **REALLY BOTHER ME.**

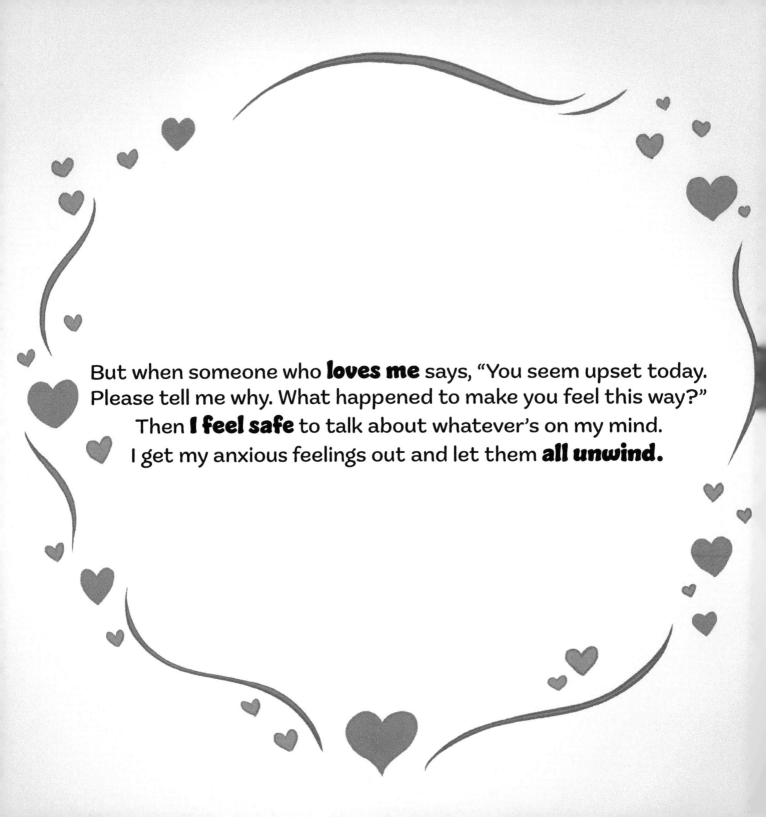

But when someone who **loves me** says, "You seem upset today.
Please tell me why. What happened to make you feel this way?"
Then **I feel safe** to talk about whatever's on my mind.
I get my anxious feelings out and let them **all unwind.**

Sometimes EVERYTHING IS FINE! My world's a happy place.
And everywhere I go I WEAR A CHEERY, SMILING FACE.

So when I feel this way, like I AM FLOATING ON A CLOUD,
I want to DANCE A JAZZY DANCE! I want to SING OUT LOUD!

And when someone who **loves me** says, "You're feeling great today. Please tell me why. What happened to make you feel this way?" Then I can **share my gladness.** And guess what I have found? **My good mood is contagious! I can spread it all around!**

I want to be **that someone** for someone else someday,
Who knows **I really like them** and think that they're okay,
Who trusts that **they can tell me anything** they want to say.
I hope that they will **do the same** for someone else someday!

Activity Page!

Read the questions and write down your answers on a piece of paper.
How is this person feeling?
Have you ever felt the same way?
What did you do when you felt like that?.
What else could you do to help your feelings unwind?

1.

2.

3.

7.

8.

9.

Word Bank

Excited   Happy   Loved   Frustrated   Crabby   Upset

Cheery   Lonely   Scared   Understood   Worried   Angry

Content   Included   Comforted   Relieved

Dear reader, please feel free to copy these activity pages to help when leading discussions.

4.

5.

6.

10.

11.

12.

Published by Orange Hat Publishing 2023
ISBN 9781645385288

Copyright © 2023 by Ruth Anfinson Bures
All Rights Reserved
I'm So Glad There's Someone
Written by Ruth Anfinson Bures
Illustrated by Amy Kleinhans

www.orangehatpublishing.com

Dedication & Acknowledgements

For Libby, Aiden, Josie, Grant,
Malachi, Oriana and Nadia.

I deeply appreciate the support and encouragement given to me by my husband, Frank, sons Frank, Bob and Joe, their wives, Bridgit, Karen, and Ana, and many friends and acquaintances who know my work. Sincere thanks to the dedicated staff at Orange Hat Publishing for making this book become a reality.

Ingram Content Group UK Ltd.
Milton Keynes UK
UKHW050047150323
418416UK00030B/38

9 781645 385288